A HEART'S HOME

This Large Print Book carries the
Seal of Approval of N.A.V.H.

A JOURNEY OF THE HEART, BOOK 6

A HEART'S HOME

COLLEEN COBLE

THORNDIKE PRESS

A part of Gale, Cengage Learning

GALE
CENGAGE Learning·

Farmington Hills, Mich • San Francisco • New York • Waterville, Maine
Meriden, Conn • Mason, Ohio • Chicago

GALE
CENGAGE Learning®

Thorndike Press® Large Print Christian Historical Fiction.
The text of this Large Print edition is unabridged.
Other aspects of the book may vary from the original edition.
Set in 19 pt. Plantin.

LIBRARY OF CONGRESS CATALOGING-IN-PUBLICATION DATA

Coble, Colleen.
  A heart's home / by Colleen Coble. — Large print edition.
    pages cm. — (A journey of the heart) (Thorndike Press large print Christian historical fiction)
    ISBN 978-1-4104-8112-2 (hardcover) — ISBN 1-4104-8112-3 (hardcover)
    1. Large type books. I. Title.
  PS3553.O2285H433 2015b
  813'.54—dc23   2015026364

Published in 2015 by arrangement with Thomas Nelson, Inc., a division of HarperCollins Christian Publishing, Inc.

Printed in Mexico
1 2 3 4 5 6 7 19 18 17 16 15

*In memory of my brother
Randy Rhoads, who taught
me to love the mountains of
Wyoming, and my grandparents
Everett and Eileen Everroad,
who loved me unconditionally.
May you walk those heavenly
mountains with joy.*

A LETTER FROM
THE AUTHOR

Dear Reader,

I can't tell you how excited I am to share this story with you! It's the first series I ever wrote, and it will always be special to me because writing was how I dealt with my brother Randy's death. You'll see a piece of my dear brother in Rand's character throughout this series. These four books were originally titled *Where Leads the Heart* and *Plains of Promise*. They haven't been available in print form for

7

nearly ten years, so I'm thrilled to share them with you.

When my brother Randy was killed in a freak lightning accident, I went to Wyoming to see where he had lived. Standing on the parade ground at Fort Laramie, the idea for the first book dropped into my head. I went home excited to write it. It took a year to write, and I thought for sure there would be a bidding war on it! ☺ Not so much. It took six more years for a publisher to pick it up. But the wait was worth it!

This series seemed a good one to break up into a serialization model to introduce readers to my work. Even in my early stories, I had to have villains and danger lurking around the corner. ☺ I hope you enjoy this trip back in time with me.

E-mail me at colleen@colleen coble.com and let me know what you think!

Love,
Colleen

ONE

December 18, 1866, Fort Phil Kearny, Wyoming Territory

The little fort in the wilderness bustled with activity outside the kitchen window. The distant sound of the post band practicing mingled with the sound of soldiers practicing maneuvers on the parade ground.

Emmie Croftner carefully slid a pie into the oven to bake. "I need to change. Isaac will be here any minute." She felt like hugging herself. "I still can't believe I'm going to be married." She handed Sarah's little brother, Joel, a cinnamon-crusted bit of raw pie dough.

At ten, he was a nearly bottom-less pit. He grinned and wolfed it down. "Can I come eat at your place sometimes?"

Sarah laughed and cuffed his head. "Only if you want to insult your only sister."

"Ow." He grinned and rubbed his reddish-gold hair, very much like Sarah's. "I like your cooking fine, but Emmie makes the best pie."

Sarah rolled her green eyes. "Okay, you're forgiven this time, but only because you're right."

A rap sounded at the door, and Emmie put her hands on her hot cheeks. "Oh dear, I'm not ready." She hurried through the kitchen to the parlor and threw open the front door to stare up into Isaac Liddle's dear face. A bit of snow covered the shoulders of his wool coat and dotted his auburn mustache with white.

"You're early." She touched a dark-brown lock that had fallen from atop her head. She rubbed floury hands on her apron. "Come in out of the cold."

The scent of wet snow followed him inside. "Let me help you off with your coat." She took his greatcoat over closer to the fire. "Sit down. Supper won't be for a little while."

He caught at her hand when she

came back and pulled her down beside him on the sofa. "You haven't changed your mind, have you?" Melting snow dripped off his hair onto the shirt covering his broad shoulders.

"Never." Isaac wasn't the rogue Monroe, her so-called "husband," had been. He was true and good.

His grin beamed. "I'm one lucky fellow." His hand went to his pocket, and he drew out a folded paper. "I wanted to show you something. It's going to be our home."

Her pulse kicked at the thought of a real home, one with her and Isaac. Rand and Sarah had made her feel welcome, but having her own place would be so very different.

She unfolded the stiff paper and looked down at the pencil drawing. "You drew this?"

He shook his head and traced the outline of the roof with his finger. "A friend did it for me."

She studied the sweet little house with its steep roof and windows. "It looks lovely."

"He's made it so we can easily add on as we have more children. See, here and here we can expand in both directions."

She touched her belly where the babe had yet to quicken. A houseful of children would suit her just fine. And she would love and care for them with all her heart. "You'll be a good father, unlike my own."

His blue eyes darkened. "I'll give

you a real home, Emmie. I promise."

"I know," she whispered. "I'm
counting on that. Um, there's
something I want to tell you." She
opened her mouth to tell him the
secret that weighed so heavily on
her heart, but Sarah came to the
doorway.

"The pie is ready."

Emmie rose quickly. It could wait
for another time.

Isaac couldn't stop smiling as he
tromped through the heavy snow
to the corral to lead a woodcutting
detail. The light in Emmie's eyes as
she'd looked at the home he
planned to build her kept him
warm.

Although the sky was clear, the trek was slow going, with huge drifts of snow left by the blizzard. Several lines of enlisted men tramped the snow down for the horses. Without their assistance, the animals would have been walking through chest-high snow in some places.

Isaac sat atop his horse and watched the surrounding hills for signs of trouble. The sun shone down on the plains and glimmered on the distant snow-topped hills. It was so different from Texas. The mountains and cool air spoke to him.

The men had only felled one tree and begun to cut it up when the whoops of a war band pierced the air as they charged over the hill to his right.

"Take cover!" He slid off his horse and flung himself down behind a rock outcropping. The soldiers were outnumbered by at least three to one. Even with the repeating rifles some of them had, they would soon be overwhelmed. He knew the lookout on Pilot Knob could see the battle, but Colonel Carrington would need at least fifteen minutes to muster the men and come to the rescue.

Emmie hummed as she washed the last of the breakfast dishes and cleaned up the pie-making mess. The wind howled around the eaves of the house, and snow clung to the outsides of the window, even sifting through the cracks to the inside sill. But the inclement weather didn't stop the singing in her heart.

Mrs. Isaac Liddle. Her new life would be here in a month.

Sarah hung the skillet on a hook over the stove and smiled. "You're looking very pleased with yourself. I'm so happy for you."

"I still can't believe it." Emmie's smile faltered. "But I'm worried about Jessica. What if she tells Isaac?"

"Tell him first."

"I started to tell him when he was here but was interrupted. I'll tell him when he gets back." Emmie lifted her head as she heard the volley of shots in the distance. She put a hand to her pounding heart. Isaac was out with the wood detail.

With Sarah on her heels, Emmie rushed through the kitchen to the parlor door and threw it open. Men ran from the parade ground to the saddled horses. Rand and Jake Campbell rode past in the first company of cavalry led by Lieutenant Fetterman.

They had grown accustomed to the wagon bringing in dead and wounded men daily. She couldn't bear the thought that Isaac's body may be brought in bristling with arrows. Now that she had finally admitted how she felt, she couldn't help fearing that he would be taken from her.

She would feel better if they had

something to do besides worrying. "Let's go see if we can do anything for Amelia."

Sarah nodded. "I'm still worried about her. It was such a hard labor. She shouldn't be home alone."

But their fears were unfounded. Amelia was sitting up in bed with her black hair brushed, a clean nightgown on, and the baby nestled in her arms. She looked up from her inspection of baby Gabrielle as they tiptoed into the room.

"What is all the excitement about?" Amelia asked with a worried frown. "I heard the men shouting and the trumpet calling assembly."

"Nothing for you to worry about." Sarah stroked a soothing hand on her friend's forehead. "Just a little skirmish with the Sioux." She frowned. "You seem a little warm. How are you feeling?"

"I'm fine." Amelia looked down at the sleeping infant. "I can't believe she's really here. Isn't she the most beautiful thing you've ever seen? I just knew I would have a baby girl."

Emmie leaned down beside her and touched the little one's face. "She's wonderful. You're so blessed. It'll seem like such a long time before my baby comes now that you have her. Sarah and I will probably wear out our welcome in the first week."

"Don't count on it." Amelia smiled. "I can never see too much of you." She sat up a little straighter and patted the side of the bed. "Sit down both of you and tell me all the fort news. Have you heard from home lately? What has Jessica been up to?"

Emmie sat on one side of the bed, and Sarah pulled the cracked straight-backed chair closer to the bed and sat down.

Emmie smiled. "Well, I do have some exciting news."

"Don't tell me. Let me guess." Amelia looked into Emmie's eyes. "You're engaged to Isaac."

Emmie gaped at her and Amelia burst out laughing. "I'm not a mind reader. Jacob told me last night." She leaned forward and hugged Emmie. "I'm so happy for both of you. Isaac is a wonderful man."

"God is very good to me," Emmie said softly. "I just hope I don't disappoint Isaac." She stood and walked to the window. "How well do we really know someone else? I'm not very brave, you know. I'm just afraid that when Isaac gets to know me better, he'll wish he had married someone else. And how will he react when he knows I was never really married to Monroe?"

Sarah stepped up behind her and turned Emmie around to face her. "You're not to think like that any- more. Isaac is no fool. He knows you well enough now to know you aren't a loose woman."

Emmie smiled, then nodded. "I'll

try to keep that in mind."

"When is the wedding?" Amelia asked.

"January eleventh. It's Rand's birthday. He'll give me away."

Amelia's face brightened. "I'll be back to normal by then. Too bad Gabrielle won't be bigger. She could be in the bridal party."

Emmie went back to the bed and touched the baby's face with one finger. The infant's skin was petal soft. "She'll be there and that's good enough for me. You certainly had us frightened."

Amelia sighed and adjusted her blankets. "I had some kind of silly premonition that I was going to die. I'm just so thankful it's over and we're both all right."

Sarah took her friend's hand. "We wouldn't let anything happen to you. You're too special to us."

Amelia squeezed Sarah's hand. "Sometimes God decrees otherwise," she said softly.

Sarah leaned over and kissed the baby. "We'd better be getting back. We'll return and bring you some nice soup for lunch. Need anything else before we go?"

Amelia shook her head. "I think I'll take a little nap while Gabrielle is sleeping." She snuggled down into the blankets.

"I'll put her in the cradle so you can rest better." Emmie gently took the baby and got her settled beside the bed.

Jacob had spent many evenings

carving a woodland scene on the cradle. Bunnies frolicked among flowers in a meadow, beautifully done. Emmie tucked the blankets around Gabrielle, then followed Sarah out of the room.

Emmie checked the fire and made sure it had enough wood before she and Sarah hurried across the parade ground toward the sutler's store. The wood detail had been gone nearly an hour. Any news of their fate would be known at the store.

It teemed with soldiers and other wives. Sarah saw Frances Grummond standing by the counter. Frances, a petite brunette with a sweet Southern accent, waved and immediately made her way toward them.

She clutched at Emmie's arm and burst into tears. "I'm so frightened. Lieutenant Smith says Fetterman took a company of infantry and one of cavalry to the relief of the wood detail, while Colonel Carrington and George went with a small detachment to cut off the Indians' retreat. But the scouts say our men were heavily outnumbered. At least one officer has been killed and several more men wounded. No one knows who yet."

The lump in Emmie's throat threatened to choke her. She couldn't lose Isaac, not when she'd just found him. Rand and Jacob were in danger too, and every woman in the room felt the same fear.

Sarah invited Frances back to their quarters to await any further news. The day passed in fitful periods of conversation. A pall of fear hung over all three women as they tried to keep up their spirits. They sang hymns, took meals to Amelia, worked with Sarah's little brother, Joel, on his studies, and above all prayed. Finally, at about nine o'clock in the evening, the bugle sounded the return of the troops. The women hastily threw on cloaks and hats and hurried across the parade ground to greet the returning soldiers.

Emmie watched fearfully as the men filed through. Their faces were tense and red from the cold wind.

Sarah cried out in relief as she spotted Rand, then Jacob. Emmie strained her eyes in the dark, trying to see a familiar set of shoulders. Where was Isaac? She scanned the crowd again. There he was. Tears of thanksgiving welled up as he turned and saw her. He smiled and waved. The men couldn't speak with them for some time, but at least they were safe.

"No-o-o!"

Emmie turned at the drawn-out wail. Mrs. DuBois screamed and beat at her daughter's restraining arms that held her from rushing to the ambulance.

"Major DuBois must be the officer who was killed," Sarah whispered.

Emmie wanted to offer her condolences, but Jessica wouldn't welcome them. At least not yet. It was hard to believe that the strong, vibrant major had been felled by a Sioux arrow.

Isaac headed her way, but Mrs. DuBois and Jessica intercepted him. Emmie's stomach tightened as she watched Jessica burst into tears and throw herself into his arms. Emmie started toward them, but Jessica pulled back and grabbed his hand, then led him away with them. He glanced back toward Emmie with a helpless expression but followed after the two weeping women.

Emmie clutched her hands together and turned to go with Sarah.

It meant nothing. He was just doing his duty. But what if Jessica told him Emmie's secret before she could?

Jessica shut the door behind Isaac, and he helped her remove her coat. He handed it to their striker, then helped Mrs. DuBois as she shrugged off her coat. "I'm so sorry for your loss."

What must Emmie have thought to see him go off like that? It had been his duty to see to his superior officer's family, and he'd respected the major. He hoped she could understand his situation. He followed the women into the parlor where a fire blazed and began to thaw his cold hands and feet. He'd been in the frigid weather for hours.

Mrs. DuBois had finally stopped crying. "I shall see about some food and hot coffee for you, Lieutenant. You look hungry and cold."

He held his hands out to the comforting heat of the flame. "Thank you, ma'am, I wouldn't turn it down."

Jessica sank onto the sofa. "I can't believe Father is gone. What will we do?"

He turned to face her and found her staring at him as if he were her last hope in the world. "Do you have family back east?"

"I would suffocate back there now. I expect Mother will return to her sister's home though. She's always hated it here."

33

Her fixed stare made him shuffle, and he wished he could make an escape. All he wanted was to see Emmie, to hold her and remember he was alive yet another day.

She wet her lips. "Isaac, have you thought of taking a wife? You could go far in the army with the right helper at your side."

He crossed his arms over his chest. "Actually, I have. I plan to marry Emmie Croftner. I asked her last night. I hope you'll wish me well."

Jessica inhaled, and moisture gleamed in her eyes. She inclined her head. "I think you should get to know her a little better before you tie the knot. There's something you don't know about her."

"I know everything I need to know." Did this have anything to do with the secret Emmie had said she must tell him? And how would Jessica know?

Mrs. DuBois returned with a plate of sandwiches and cups of steaming coffee. If there was something problematic in Emmie's past, he wanted to hear it from her lips.

Two

Emmie barely closed her eyes all night. She kept expecting to hear Sioux war cries as they attacked the fort.

As soon as breakfast was over, she went to grab her cloak. "Let's pay our respects to Mrs. DuBois and Jessica."

Emmie's heart pounded and her mouth was dry as she and Sarah went across the parade ground to the major's quarters. Jessica was sure to have heard the news of the engagement by now. How would she react?

Isaac had gone out on duty first thing this morning, and she longed to tell him her secret. He wasn't anything like Monroe, and she prayed he would understand her dead husband had been no husband at all. She'd been gullible, oh so gullible.

Mrs. DuBois's striker answered the door and ushered them into the parlor. Most of the officers employed "strikers," enlisted men who worked for them as servants on off-duty hours for a small compensation. Emmie had asked why Rand hadn't done the same instead of taking in a homeless waif like her. It was probably more expensive to pay for her expenses than to employ a striker. But Sarah had told her that Rand thought Sarah needed the company more than the physical help.

Jessica, sitting alone and staring out the window, looked up as they entered the room. Her eyes, swollen from crying, narrowed as she saw Emmie. "What do you want? Did you come here to gloat? You have everything you want."

Emmie flinched. "We just want you to know how sorry we are about your father. I would like to be your friend, Jessica. Not your enemy. I never meant to hurt you."

Her face flushing with rage, Jessica rose and advanced toward them. "Get out! I don't want your condolences, and I certainly don't need your friendship."

Emmie swallowed hard and put out a trembling hand to Jessica. "I've been praying for you. I don't know what hurt drives you so, but God does."

Jessica's eyes filled with tears, but then her face hardened and she flushed a deeper red. "Get out!" She advanced toward them. "Get out — get out — get out!" She screamed the words at them. "I don't need your pity!"

Emmie and Sarah backed away hastily. "We truly are sorry," Sarah said as they slipped out through the door. "We didn't come just to be polite."

As the door shut in their faces,

Emmie and Sarah looked at each other. Sarah was pale, and Emmie was sure she looked just as ravaged as her friend did.

"You know, I think you have a lot of insight," Sarah said a few minutes later as they drew near their house. "I never really thought about why Jessica is like she is. There must be some hidden pain in her life that has shaped her."

Emmie nodded, her gaze on a familiar set of shoulders. "There's Isaac." She raised her gloved hand, and he altered his course and headed their way.

"I'll see you at the house." Sarah waved at Isaac and took off briskly toward Officers' Row.

He reached Emmie. His face was

reddened from the cold. "There you are. How are they holding up?"

"As poorly as you'd expect. It's so sad." She saw his worried glance toward the DuBois residence. His kindness was one of the many things she loved about him.

"I've got to go out with the men. You said there was something you wanted to tell me?"

Why was he bringing it up now? Had Jessica already told him? Emmie searched his expression but couldn't discern any suspicion.

"There will be time later." She squeezed his hand. "Hurry back home to me."

"I will." He pulled the house plans from inside his coat and pressed them into her hand. "You keep these and think of any changes you want."

She clutched the paper and tucked it into her reticule where the wind couldn't snatch it away. The thought of a home with Isaac was the one bright spot in this tragic day.

Emmie blew a strand of hair out of her eyes. Baking pies had heated up the kitchen quite nicely this afternoon. She set the mincemeat pie on the table and cut a piece for Sarah. "See if it's any good."

Sarah tasted it. "It's delicious! Let's take some to Amelia."

"Should we wait for Morning Song to return from the Indian encampment?"

Sarah shook her head. "She won't be back until this evening."

The women bundled up in warm cloaks and hurried toward Amelia's quarters. The wind snatched Emmie's breath away as soon as they stepped outside. As they approached Jake and Amelia's small cabin, they heard the baby's wail. The infant sounded frantic, and Emmie hastened her steps. What could be wrong with little Gabrielle?

They didn't bother to knock but opened the door and hurried to the bedroom, where the baby shrieked in her cradle. Amelia lay on the floor beside the bed, one arm reaching toward her tiny daughter.

"Amelia!" Sarah knelt beside her.

"Quick, help me get her back into bed." She grasped Amelia's shoulders and Emmie lifted her legs. They managed to place her on the bed.

Emmie touched Amelia's skin. "She's burning up! You take care of Gabrielle, and I'll fetch Dr. Horton."

Emmie flew out the door and across the parade ground. By the time she and the doctor returned, Sarah had managed to calm the baby with a cloth dipped in sugar water. The baby was sucking on it vigorously and making mewing sounds of contentment.

Dr. Horton frowned when he felt the heat radiating off Amelia's body. He quickly put his stethoscope to her chest and listened intently. Amelia muttered incoherently and moved restlessly in the bed.

"What is it?" Sarah bit her lip.

The doctor put his instruments away. "Pneumonia, I'm afraid. Her condition is very grave. We must try to reduce the fever. You need to sponge her down with tepid water. She won't like it, but it must be done."

Emmie nodded. "I'll do it while you take care of the baby."

Sarah nodded. "When Morning Song gets back, we can send her to the sutler's store for some tinned milk."

Emmie warmed a pan of water to lukewarm and began to sponge

Amelia's body. *Wring, wipe, wring, wipe.* Over and over, Emmie wiped the damp cloth over Amelia. After an hour, Emmie felt as though her arms would fall off. But still her friend drifted in and out of consciousness, calling for Jacob and baby Gabrielle.

When Amelia finally fell into a fitful sleep, Emmie stepped outside the bedroom to speak with Morning Song and Sarah. Gabrielle wailed and wouldn't suck the cloth dipped in tinned milk anymore.

Morning Song had tears in her eyes. "I have extra milk if you wish me to feed her."

Sarah quickly handed her the baby. "I wanted to ask earlier but I didn't want to make you uncomfortable."

"Hearing her cries hurts me when I could help." Morning Song turned away to nurse the baby by the fire.

The doctor came in again, and Emmie followed him into the bedroom with Sarah on her heels. He listened to Amelia's chest again, then stepped back, his expression grave. "Unchanged. It's very serious. I've sent someone to fetch Jacob, but he hasn't returned yet."

Morning Song slipped in behind Emmie. She had a cup of steaming liquid in her hands. "I wish to try some Sioux medicine. It is from the bark of a tree you call white oak."

"Go ahead. There's nothing much I can do." Dr. Horton stepped toward the door. "I'll be back in an hour or so."

Emmie lifted Amelia's head and shoulders onto her lap while Morning Song spooned the steaming liquid into her mouth. Some ran out the corners of her mouth, but she managed to swallow a little. Emmie wiped Amelia's mouth and eased her back against the pillows.

Sarah wrung her hands. "I wish Jacob would get back. I'm so afraid."

Amelia moaned and both women knelt beside her bed. She opened her eyes and they looked bright and blue against the pure white of her face. Those blue eyes shone with love and a strange joy. Emmie swallowed hard and fought a rising sense of panic as Amelia smiled at someone just past Emmie's shoulder. Emmie almost turned around to look, but she knew no one was there.

"Tell Jacob I'll be waiting for him," Amelia whispered. "I'm sorry I have to leave him alone."

"No, no." Sarah shook her head. "Don't talk like that. Jacob will be here soon and you'll be fine."

"You must be strong, Sarah." Amelia's voice was a soft croak. "Help Jacob all you can and tell him I love him."

She coughed violently, then lay gasping for air. She looked again at a spot just to the side of Emmie, stretched out her arms, and closed her eyes. She gave one last little sigh, a strange little hiccup, and her chest grew still. Baby Gabrielle wailed suddenly as though she somehow knew her mother was gone.

"No!" Sarah wailed. She tried to pull Amelia to a sitting position, but she was limp and unresponsive.

Emmie took Sarah by the shoulders and pulled her close. She swallowed hard past the tears burning in her throat. How could this be?

She leaned her forehead against Sarah's head and closed her eyes as Sarah cried out in sudden comprehension of the loss of her best friend. Morning Song hurried to tend to the crying baby. Emmie heard her clucking noises of comfort through the dull veil of grief that squeezed her heart.

"She's gone," she whispered against Sarah's hair. "But we know she's with the Lord."

"She can't be dead," Sarah said numbly. "She can't be. We've always been there for each other. This can't be true. Call the doctor." But the words were said without any real conviction.

They clung together for several unbelieving minutes, then Emmie pulled away and stood. She looked down at Sarah's white face and held out her hand.

Sarah shook her head. "I want to stay here for just a few minutes," she said with a pleading look. "I just want to remember the good times we had when we were growing up." Her words were choked with tears. "I still can't believe she's gone."

Emmie squeezed her shoulder, then left her alone with Amelia.

Morning Song was in the kitchen with little Gabrielle. Emmie put water on to boil for some tea, then sat wearily beside Morning Song. Young John played happily on the floor with some wooden blocks, and Emmie's gaze lingered on her little nephew.

"I don't know how to tell Jacob," Emmie whispered.

She could only imagine the pain he would feel. And he had a new baby to care for. Of course they would all help, but it was still a huge responsibility to raise a child alone. Emmie gulped as she thought about the situation.

Her promise to Amelia.

She'd promised her friend she would marry Jake and care for Gabrielle if anything happened. Surely Amelia wouldn't expect her to keep a promise like that now that Emmie had found Isaac.

She bit her lip and blinked back more tears. Just when life seemed so perfect, everything fell apart. How could any of them look forward to the wedding when Amelia was gone? Even the thought of that sweet little house seemed impossible in the face of this tragedy.

The day dragged by somehow. Morning Song took the children

home to Sarah's, while Sarah and Emmie washed Amelia's cold, still body and dressed her in her favorite Sunday dress, the violet one that deepened the color of her eyes. Emmie couldn't bear the thought of those extraordinary eyes never widening in wonder again. Sarah combed and dressed her friend's long dark hair one last time as her tears gently bathed Amelia's white but still-beautiful face. As the sad news traveled around the post, several ladies dropped by with whispers of condolences and offerings of food.

The bugle finally announced the men's return to the fort, but it was nearly an hour before they heard the heavy tread of the men on the front porch. Isaac and Rand each held Jacob's arms as they practically carried him through the door. His face was slack and glazed with disbelief and an overwhelming grief. All three men bore signs of the tears they'd shed.

Isaac's eyes were full of sorrow as they met Emmie's, and he opened his arms to her. Sarah uttered a tiny cry and flew into Rand's arms, and they all wept together as Jacob stumbled toward the room where his wife lay.

Moments later, they heard his harsh sobs as he sank to the floor beside Amelia. Emmie's eyes filled with tears again. Isaac pulled her closer and rested his chin on the top of her head as she sobbed against his chest. His shirt smelled of cold air and the warm musk of his male scent. She felt loved and comforted in the circle of his arms with his breath warm on her face. But the grief and aloneness poor Jake must be feeling.

After a little while, the four of them tiptoed into the bedroom to be with Jake. His sobs had stilled, but his fingers still traced the contours of Amelia's face. Rand put his hand on his younger brother's shoulder.

"I never got to say good-bye," Jacob choked out. "How could she leave without saying good-bye?"

Sarah knelt beside him. "Her last words were for you. She said, 'Tell Jacob I'll be waiting for him. Tell him I love him.' "

Jacob groaned and buried his face in his hands. His shoulders shook with the intensity of his grief. After a few moments, he lifted his head. "Where's the baby? Is she all right?"

"She's fine," Emmie said. "Morning Song took her to our house along with John and Joel."

"I want her. She's all I have left of Amelia now."

"I'll go get her." Emmie started to leave but Isaac stopped her.

"The wind is terrible. Let me go."

Emmie shook her head. "I want to. I'll be fine." She wrapped her cloak about her and stepped out into the wind-whipped snow. She was numb from the emotions of the day as she hurried across the parade ground. The wind stung her cheeks, and the prickle of feeling brought a new wave of grief. How would they all bear this?

Morning Song looked up as Emmie stumbled into the parlor. Little Gabrielle and John slept contentedly on the cot. Joel dozed with his head against Morning Song's knee. The baby slept so peacefully. Emmie's heart clenched with love for the motherless mite. Amelia would have been such a wonderful mother. Now Gabrielle would never know the lovely person who had given her life. Tears stung her eyes as the baby stirred and opened blue eyes so very like her mother's.

"Jake is back and wants to see the

baby." Emmie knelt beside the cot and gently bundled the blankets around the baby. She lifted the baby into her arms and looked at Morning Song for a moment. "He's taking it very hard."

Morning Song nodded. "I knew it would be so. When one is cut, the other bleeds. I should come too?"

Emmie shook her head. "You stay with the boys. There's no sense in making them come out in this cold. When we get back, maybe you could go over and feed her."

"I will come."

There was a thread of emotion Emmie didn't recognize in Morning Song's voice. The young woman was so stoic most of the time. It was hard to guess what she felt and how strongly Amelia's death was affecting her.

With a last glance at her friend, Emmie pulled the blanket over Gabrielle's face and tucked her under her cloak for added warmth. The wind caught the door out of her fingers, but Morning Song was behind her to grab it and pull it shut.

Jacob was waiting at the door when she stomped the snow off her feet on the porch. He took the bundled baby out of her arms as soon as she extricated her from under the cloak. With tender hands, he pulled back the blankets and gazed into his daughter's tiny face. She yawned and opened her blue eyes.

"You look so much like your mama," Jacob whispered. "Thank God." He pulled her close, then went to the bedroom and shut the door.

Emmie sank wearily onto the cot in the parlor.

Isaac put a hand on her shoulder and squeezed gently. "We'll get through this. God is here and in control."

Emmie nodded. She knew it was so. But why would God allow such sorrow to come to them? She didn't know if she would ever understand.

THREE

The day of the funeral dawned clear and cold. December twentieth, just five days before Christmas. The wind wasn't as fierce as usual, which was a mercy from God. Jacob was insistent that the baby be at the service, although she was much too tiny to be out in the weather. Emmie bundled her carefully, then followed Sarah and Rand to the little chapel. Isaac was waiting for her outside the door.

"I've been praying for you all

morning." He squeezed her hand. "For all of us."

Emmie nodded in gratitude. "Rand was at Jacob's all night. Morning Song too. She insisted she should be the one to go since she is feeding the baby. Poor little John looks so bewildered. He doesn't understand what his mama is doing with that other baby all the time."

She eased onto the bench beside Sarah and Rand. Jacob sat on the other side of his brother. He stared down at his hands with such a look of suffering that Emmie's eyes filled with fresh tears. She ached to comfort him somehow, but only God could give him the peace he needed.

Reverend Howard cleared his throat as he nervously glanced around at the packed building. The entire garrison had turned out to see Amelia put to rest. "Today is a day of mourning for us gathered here to pay our final respects to Amelia Campbell." He leaned forward slightly over the pulpit. "But I say to all of you that it is a day of great rejoicing as well."

Jacob glanced up sharply with a frown.

"Our dear sister showed God's love to everyone she knew. Some of you may wish to tell about how Amelia demonstrated her love for her God in your own lives."

He sat down and the chapel was silent. Then one by one people stood and told of kindnesses that Amelia had shared. Tears rained down Emmie's cheeks as she listened to the outpouring of love. Jacob sobbed when one soldier told how he had popped a button on his coat while carrying in a load of wood for Amelia, and she insisted on sewing it back on and then gave him some tea and buttered bread.

The chapel was silent for a few moments, and Reverend Howard stood again. "I think we can all heartily agree that Amelia Campbell lived her life to the fullest. She loved her family and she loved her fellow man. I pray that each one of us can impact lives the way she did."

As Emmie, clinging to Isaac's

arm, followed the procession to the grave, her heart was lighter than she would have dreamed possible. She could only imagine the joy Amelia was feeling at this moment. How could she mourn when she thought of her friend's unimaginable bliss? A glance at Jacob's face showed he did not share her thoughts. Grief was etched deeply in his face as he carried his daughter through the ankle-deep snow.

The service at graveside was brief, just the traditional ashes to ashes, dust to dust eulogy. They hurried home through the increasing wind. Emmie felt a sense of uneasiness as she followed Jacob's broad back. He seemed hard and angry. She knew he blamed God. When the minister had tried to offer words of comfort, he had turned away with a harsh, "Don't talk to me of God's grace and mercy. My wife is dead and my daughter is motherless." She had never expected an attitude like that from Jacob. Amelia had said he had a strong faith.

"Emmie, would you mind coming in a moment?" Jacob said as they reached his quarters. "I need to talk to you."

"Of course." She lifted her face toward Isaac, and he brushed his lips across her cheek.

She smiled and squeezed his hand before following Jacob inside. She hung her cloak on a hook in the hall and hurried to the kitchen to boil some water for tea. She was cold clear through and Jacob had to be as well.

He put little Gabrielle on the bed and sat at the kitchen table while Emmie rummaged through the open shelves for some teacups. He sat silently while she finished preparing the tea. She glanced over at him once or twice and felt a little intimidated by his grim look.

"Sugar?" she asked. He shook his head and took the steaming cup. She dropped sugar in her own cup and sat beside him at the table.

"You aren't going to like what I have to say," he said abruptly. "I need your help."

Emmie smiled at him. Was that all this was about? "You know I'll help in any way I can. I loved

Amelia too. I know it will be hard to take care of Gabrielle by yourself."

"I need more than just occasional help. Gabrielle needs a full-time mother. I don't want her growing up shifted from place to place like a homeless puppy."

Emmie's smile faltered. "You want me to take her? Don't you want her to live with you?"

Jacob scowled. "I wouldn't give my daughter up for anything. She's the only important thing in my life. I don't want you to take her to live with you. I want you to live here with me and take care of her."

"Jacob, I would do anything I could to help, but I can't stay here alone with you. The entire fort would talk."

"Not if we were married. I want you to honor your promise to Amelia."

The words hammered into her brain and Emmie sat back as though from a blow. Honor her promise? She couldn't marry Jacob! She was going to marry Isaac. Kind, loving Isaac who was waiting for her at Sarah's.

She shook her head. "You can't be serious. You know I'm going to marry Isaac."

"I know you are a woman of your word and Gabrielle needs a mother. You needn't worry about me bothering you or expecting anything else from you except to take care of my daughter. I'll never love another woman like I loved Amelia. You'll look after Gabrielle, fix my meals, and tend to the house. That's all. You and the baby can have the bedroom. I'll sleep on the cot in the parlor. When she's a little older, I'll release you and you can marry Isaac."

He stared at her fiercely as he said the words. His stern look seemed to dare her to contradict his command. Emmie swallowed hard. What should she do? Didn't he know how unreasonable his demand was? Did he really expect her to give up her life and future with the man she loved to be an unloved nursemaid and housekeeper?

You made a promise, a voice inside her head whispered.

Jake stood up abruptly. "I know this is a shock, so I'm going to leave you. I need to talk to the colonel for a little while. You think it over. I know you'll do the right thing."

The right thing? This was supposed to be the right thing? Emmie stared at his back as he strode toward the door. How could he ask such a thing of her? What should she do?

She twisted her hands in her lap and stared at the sleeping baby. Amelia had been such a dear friend. Surely she wouldn't expect Emmie to give up her own chance at happiness to take care of the stern man Jacob had become.

A timid knock at the door broke into her confused thoughts. Jacob pulled it open, and Morning Song stood on the other side with a colorful Sioux blanket around her shoulders.

Jake stepped aside. "Gabrielle is still sleeping. I very much appreciate what you've been doing for me and the baby, Morning Song."

She stared at the floor and color flooded her cheeks. "I would do anything for you and Gabrielle."

He put his hand on Morning Song's shoulder. "Thank you." He stepped around her, opened the door, and pulled it shut behind him.

Emmie gestured to the table. "Would you like some tea while we wait for Gabrielle to wake up?" She needed someone to talk to, someone impartial.

Morning Song nodded. "Tea sounds good. The winter wind is very bad." She looked into Emmie's eyes. "My friend is not happy. This place is sad for you."

"Yes, but that's not the only problem. I don't know what to do about Jacob." She stood and put the kettle on the woodstove, then sat and clenched her hands in her lap. "I made a promise to Amelia. One that I never thought I would have to keep."

"My father says if a warrior cannot keep his word in the camp, do not trust him in battle with the enemy."

"But what if keeping that word will ruin the person's life?" Emmie blinked back the moisture in her eyes as she gazed pleadingly at Morning Song. "I made the promise without thinking. But it was only to ease Amelia's agitation. I never expected to have to do what she asked." The kettle whistled, and she went to the stove and poured the boiling water into the teapot, then brought it to the table.

Morning Song watched her prepare the tea for a moment. "What have you said you will do?" She touched Emmie's hand.

"Several weeks ago Amelia was distressed and convinced she wouldn't live through childbirth. She knew I was also expecting a child and was alone. So she asked me to marry Jacob so I could care for them. Then my baby and I would be provided for as well. Now Jacob expects me to honor that promise."

A strange look Emmie couldn't identify darkened Morning Song's features, then was gone. Was it anger? Dismay?

Morning Song gave a slow nod. "Your friend cared for you even when she was afraid. I see her thoughts." She took a sip of tea, then set it down carefully. "A vow is most important when it's most hard."

"I wouldn't really call it a vow." Emmie sighed. "What about Isaac? I made a promise to him too. I love him. I've been so happy these past few days . . . happier than I've ever been."

"I have seen this happiness. I cannot tell you what to do. You must seek the answer in your own spirit."

The baby whimpered in the bedroom and both women looked up. Morning Song rose to her feet. "You are strong, Emmie. You will do the right thing." She turned and went into the bedroom.

Everyone expected Emmie to be strong, but she wasn't. How could she turn her back on her love for Isaac? She rose and took her cloak from the hook by the stove. She would talk to Sarah and Rand. They would know what to do.

The wind took her breath away, and Emmie had to battle to stay on her feet across the parade ground. Her bonnet lifted from her head for a moment before she yanked it down and tied it firmly in place. Drifts of snow were beginning to pile up against the steps as she hurried onto the porch.

Sarah was curled up with a quilt and a magazine on the cot by the fire. She looked up as Emmie came into the parlor. "Your face is so red! You shouldn't be out in this wind. Come join me under this quilt."

Emmie threw off her cloak and hung it by the fireplace, then dove under the quilt. Even with the fire going full blast, the heat couldn't keep up with the wind, and the room was chilly. Her teeth chattered as she nestled close to Sarah.

"You are frozen." Sarah wrapped the quilt tightly around Emmie. "Where have you been? I expected you back long ago."

"Jacob wanted to talk to me."

"All this time? What did he want?"

Emmie drew her legs up under the quilt and leaned against the wall behind her as she shared her predicament with her friend.

"Amelia never told me that! When was this?" Sarah asked.

"Several weeks ago when she wasn't feeling well."

Sarah sat up straight. "Jacob would never agree to that! He wouldn't let someone else make such an important decision for him. Not even Amelia."

"He agreed before she ever asked

me. And now he wants me to do what Amelia asked and marry him."

Sarah was silent for a moment. "I have to admit I'm shocked. But that was before you and Isaac were engaged. Amelia would never expect you to keep a promise like that now."

"I've been thinking about it, and I think she would. When she heard about my engagement after Gabrielle was born, she said it was a good thing she made it through the birth all right so I wouldn't have to keep my promise to her." She smiled a crooked smile, though her eyes burned. "He says I wouldn't have to worry about any physical demands from him. Just take care of Gabrielle, cook, and clean. When Gabrielle is a little older, he will release me. But starting a marriage with divorce in mind doesn't seem right either."

"Does he just expect you to give up a full life with Isaac to become some kind of glorified nanny?" Sarah's voice rose in her agitation.

"I've been telling myself the same things for the past two hours. But I keep coming back to the fact that I promised Amelia. Doesn't God expect us to keep our word?"

Sarah wilted. "Yes," she murmured. Then she brightened. "But you are free from the promise if Jacob will release you."

"He won't." Emmie sighed again.

"I don't know how I'm going to tell Isaac."

FOUR

The wind chased Isaac and Rand across the parade ground to the Campbell house. Rand opened the door, the two men hurried into the room, and Rand slammed the door behind them.

He glanced from Sarah to Emmie, then bent to kiss his wife. "I'm cold clear down to my socks. Any stew left?"

"It's on the stove. I'll get it." Sarah scrambled from beneath the quilt and started toward the kitchen. "Uh, why don't you help me get it ready, Rand?" she said with a sidelong look at Emmie.

Rand looked surprised, but he followed her into the kitchen.

Isaac looked at Emmie's sad face. The entire fort felt the same way. "Looks like Sarah wanted to leave us alone." He sat beside her on the cot. He slipped an arm around her and pulled her close. "I'm so sorry, honey. I know you loved her."

Emmie sighed and nestled in the crook of his arm. She turned her face up to him and he bent his head. As his lips found hers, he drew her closer and sensed a desperation in her he'd never seen. He wanted to keep kissing her all night.

He grinned as he drew back moments later. "Are you sure we can't get married sooner?"

Emmie began to tremble in his arms. Tears pooled in her eyes. Isaac thumbed away a drop that escaped down her cheek. "I know you're hurting. I wish I could fix everything."

Emmie pulled away from him and clenched her hands together in her lap. "I must tell you something and I don't know how."

Isaac frowned. "If it's that secret you and Jessica have been talking about, it doesn't matter."

"So she *did* say something."

"She didn't tell me your secret."

Emmie gulped and swiped at the tears on her face. "That's not what I have to tell you. It's even worse."

"Just say it. I love you and nothing will change that."

"I love you too. That's what makes this so hard." She looked up and stared into his eyes. "I made a promise to Amelia, one I never expected to have to keep."

Isaac smiled in relief. "I would be glad to take her baby and love her. But I doubt that Jacob would allow it."

"Just let me finish. Amelia thought she wouldn't survive childbirth several weeks ago. This was before you and I were engaged, before I would admit even to myself how much I loved you. She asked me to give her my word that if something happened to her, I would take care of the baby and marry Jacob."

The only sound for a moment was the crackling of the fire and the banging of pots in the kitchen. Isaac felt light-headed as the words soaked in. "You promised to marry Jake?"

Emmie nodded. "And he intends to hold me to my promise." She took Isaac's hand in a desperate grip. "He says he'll release me when Gabrielle is a little older. But that means divorcing, and I'm not sure I can enter such a contract in good conscience."

Isaac was silent and pain squeezed his chest. Honor was never easy, but he'd never expected to be faced with something this hard. He pulled his hand away and stood.

"I'm going to talk to Jacob." He pulled on his greatcoat and went to the door. Turning, he stared down at her. "But even if I have to wait a few years to have a home with you, I'll do it, Emmie. I'll never abandon you. Not ever."

But even as he pulled the door closed behind him, he had a sinking feeling that nothing would ever be put right in this mess.

Isaac woke the next morning with a heavy heart as he remembered the events of the night before. He'd intended to talk to Jacob last night, but the small house was dark when he reached it. He'd talk to him today.

Reveille was already sounding as

he strode toward the stables after bolting down some hardtack in the mess hall. He saddled Buck, his buckskin gelding, and made it to the parade ground just in time for boots and saddles. He was on guard duty for the wood detail. He caught a glimpse of Rand ahead, with Jacob trailing behind several other soldiers.

There had been so many skirmishes with the Sioux lately that the guard detail numbered near ninety men to protect the wood detail. The detail followed the river, then veered off on the trail to the pinery cutting area. They had gone only a hundred yards or so when a man in front of him yelled as an arrow whistled by his ear.

Rand shouted for the men to set up the corral formation, and Isaac raced to create a protective circle with the other soldiers. Indians massed on the hills all around, and he sighed in relief as he heard the picket on Pilot Hill blow the signal that told the fort there were many Indians. Reinforcements would come from the fort soon. They just had to hold on.

Emmie heard the signal from Pilot Hill and then the sound of the bugle calling men together, but she tried not to worry. It was an almost everyday occurrence lately. A few minutes later she heard the boom of the mountain howitzer. Joel looked up at the sound, but it, too, was almost commonplace these days. The Sioux feared the "gun that shoots twice" and almost always scattered after its use.

Emmie washed and dried the dishes while Sarah dusted and made the beds. Joel carried in wood for the fire, then ran off to play with Jimmy Carrington.

Emmie was deep in her thoughts when a knock at the door startled her. "I'll get it," she called to Sarah.

Morning Song had gone to care for Gabrielle first thing this morning, and she wouldn't knock anyway, so Emmie wondered who could be out this morning as she hurried to the door.

Frances Grummond's tearstained face peered out of a fur bonnet.

"Oh, Emmie, I'm so frightened. George volunteered to go to the rescue of the wood detail, and I have such an uncanny dread on my soul. He was almost killed two weeks ago. Would you go with me to Mrs. Wands'? The other ladies are gathered there too."

"Of course we will." Emmie's heart sank. Isaac, Rand, and Jake were all with the wood detail. "Would you like some tea first?"

"No, no. I just need to be with someone. Could we go now?" Frances's voice broke as she wrung her hands.

Sarah and Emmie grabbed their cloaks and bonnets and followed Frances outside. The wind still whistled, but a weak, watery sunshine brightened the day. Frances's baby was due in just a few weeks, and Emmie worried that the strain would bring on her friend's labor. She sent up a quick prayer for Frances.

The assembled ladies looked up when Emmie, Sarah, and Frances entered the Wandses' parlor. Mrs. Carrington hurried to take Frances in her arms. "My dear, don't fret so. There is no more cause for concern than usual. We both heard my husband tell George not to cross Lodge Trail Ridge, where the Indians are likely to lie in ambush. Your husband will be all right."

"I have such a strange foreboding," Frances sobbed as she let Mrs. Carrington lead her to a chair.

Sarah and Emmie followed and sat on the sofa beside her. They all soon had steaming cups of tea and Frances began to calm down. The door pounded again and Mrs. Wands hurried to answer it.

A sergeant stood twisting his cap in his hands. "Colonel Carrington sent me to tell you ladies that the wood detail has broken corral and reached the pinery safely. But Fetterman's detail went beyond Lodge Trail Ridge."

Frances cried out at the news of the detail's disobedience of orders, and Mrs. Carrington patted her hand. "George will be all right."

Frances relaxed a bit, but she still sat on the edge of her seat. Emmie could tell she was listening to the sounds outside. They had a lunch of small sandwiches and stew, but tension still filled the room. They jumped when they heard a shout and a horse go thundering past outside, and they all grabbed their cloaks and went out to the porch.

Colonel Carrington ordered a howitzer to be readied and gave the order for a general alarm. Soldiers ran in all directions as every man in the garrison reported to the position assigned to him in an extreme emergency.

"What does it mean?" Frances cried out.

"Probably the Indians have been turned back," Mrs. Carrington said soothingly.

Rooster came scurrying up the

steps to the ladies clustered on the porch. "No need to fret, ladies. Them Sioux bucks won't get ya. I promise."

Then one of the men shouted to open the gate, and the colonel's orderly came thundering through on one of the commander's horses. "Reno Valley is full of Indians! There are several hundred on the road and to the west of it. It was a trap!"

Emmie was standing beside Frances and caught her as she sagged to the ground. "Help me!" she cried to Sarah.

The rest of the women clustered around and they got Frances inside and on Mrs. Wands's bed. Mrs. Carrington put a cold cloth to

Frances's forehead and she soon came around.

Frances sat up with a start and burst into tears. "He's dead. I know it."

"Have faith," Mrs. Carrington said. "Henry sent Captain Ten Eyck out with every man who could be spared. They'll get there in time."

They all went back to the porch. The silence was so intense it was almost painful, and suddenly several shots rang out. They listened as the shots increased to a frantic pitch, followed by a few rapid volleys, then scattering shots, and finally a dead silence.

"Captain Ten Eyck has repulsed the Indians," Mrs. Carrington said.

Colonel Carrington dashed down from the lookout. Emmie shuddered at the look of dread on his face. She looked at Sarah and saw the same dread reflected on her face. What was happening to their men?

FIVE

Isaac lay behind a rock outcropping. They had made it safely to the pinery, but without reinforcements, they would never make it back to the fort. Rand lay a dozen feet away behind his own rock and Jake several yards beyond his brother behind a tree. Dozens of Indians hid just beyond the rise to the west. They were too well hidden to waste his precious ammunition on. He kept a close eye on the slope as he prayed for reinforcements to be quick. He wasn't quite sure what the Sioux were waiting on. Were they playing a game? It would be dark soon and Indians didn't make war at night.

A volley of shots in the distance rang out. They increased in ferocity for several frantic minutes, then tapered off to an occasional shot before silence descended. Isaac knew a horrific battle had just taken place, but which side had won? He lifted his head cautiously, then ducked as an arrow sailed by overhead. The arrow was followed by fierce war cries as a band of Sioux rushed toward them.

Rand cried, "Hold your fire until my signal!" Several moments passed. As the band came closer, he gasped, then yelled, "Wolverine!"

The lead Sioux faltered, then pulled his pony to a stop. He shouted something at the rest of the warriors, and they stopped behind him. He gazed at the rock where Rand lay.

Rand slowly got to his feet. "No, Rand, don't," Isaac whispered.

Rand raised a hand. "Greetings, old friend. I did not think to see you again."

The Sioux dismounted and warily approached Rand.

"Hold your fire," Rand said again to his fellow soldiers. He stepped forward with his hand outstretched as the young warrior came closer.

Isaac noticed a livid scar running

down Wolverine's cheek as he stopped in front of Rand. He'd heard Sarah talk about Wolverine and the young woman he was pledged to marry. Rand had spared Wolverine's life during a battle once, and the two became blood brothers after that.

"I did not think to see my friend again." Wolverine gazed at Rand for a long moment. "I think many times of my friend with the blue coat and my vow. I watch always in battle to make sure I honor my vow never to fight with my friend."

Rand nodded. "I also watch for my warrior friend. It is good to see you."

Wolverine grunted. "You in much danger. We will drive the bluecoats from the fort by the river. Already many dead beyond the hills." He gestured toward Lodge Trail Ridge.

Isaac looked over at Jake and saw the same alarm on his face. Many killed? Was the relief party dead? What about the fort? Was Emmie safe?

Rand put a hand on Wolverine's shoulder. "What of the fort? Sarah is in the fort."

The warrior shook his head. "We not attack fort yet. But soon. You go back to fort. Other men come soon to bring you back. Then you must leave fort. I not fight with my brother."

Rand was silent a moment. "I will not fight my brother. But I cannot leave the fort unless my commander tells me to."

"Then you must tell him that the Sioux will destroy fort. We will fight to last blade and never stop until the bluecoats leave our hunting ground."

Rand's hand slid down and gripped Wolverine's hand. "God keep you safe, my brother."

Wolverine gazed into Rand's eyes. "And you, my brother." He turned and walked back to his pony. He vaulted onto his pony, then raised a hand before turning and galloping away. The rest of the band followed.

Isaac got to his feet, and he and Jacob reached Rand's side at the same time.

Rand stared at the warrior's departing figure. "I knew Wolverine was with Red Cloud, and I always have watched for him. I didn't want to ever break my vow of peace with him."

"Do you think he told you the truth about the rescue party? Could they really be dead?" Jacob asked.

The rest of the men were slowly beginning to gather around them. "Don't say anything," Rand said quietly.

A lieutenant slapped Rand on the back. "You must have done some fancy palavering with those savages. Congratulations."

"I knew him," Rand said.

"Looks like they hightailed it because of reinforcements." The lieutenant nodded toward the hill, and they turned as Captain Ten Eyck and his men thundered up to them.

Ten Eyck dismounted and ran toward them. "We drove off a band just over the hill. Is everyone all right?"

"Just fine, thanks to you." The lieutenant turned and ordered the men to round up the horses.

"Just be glad you're getting back in one piece," Captain Ten Eyck said quietly. "Fetterman's command wasn't so lucky."

"The relief party?"

Ten Eyck nodded to Rand. "Eighty-one men slaughtered and not one left alive. We drove off some Indians and recovered many bodies, but nearly half are still out there. The attack on the wood train was a decoy to draw another force out. Thousands of Sioux were hiding just over Lodge Trail Ridge."

The news was so horrific no one responded for several long moments. Eighty-one men. It was almost beyond comprehension. There had never been a slaughter like that in the Indian wars. And thousands of Sioux. Isaac couldn't imagine such a large force of warriors. Two or three hundred was usually considered a large band.

"May God have mercy on their souls," Isaac said finally. "What of the fort?"

"Safe, but we don't know for how long," Captain Ten Eyck said. "Colonel Carrington has readied every mountain howitzer and every available man. But we've been operating with a minimal force, and you know how low our ammunition is. So we'd better return as quickly as we can."

They all hurried off to mount up and get back to the fort. Isaac just wanted to see Emmie with his own eyes and make sure she was safe, and he knew Rand felt the same about Sarah. He glanced at Jacob riding beside him. Did he worry about Emmie at all?

Emmie sat with the other women around the fire in Mrs. Wands's quarters as night drew on. The wind whistled outside as the temperature dropped. Rooster had been predicting a blizzard all day, and the weather seemed to be trying to prove him right. Only a few flakes had fallen so far, but the wind was already whipping the existing snow into drifts.

The evening gun sounded, but the men still weren't back. The colonel's orderly, Sample, had come in some time ago with the news that Reno Valley was full of Indians and nothing could be seen of Fetterman. The entire fort knew some terrible disaster had taken place, but no one knew just what it was.

It was all Emmie could do to hold her terror in check. What if Isaac had been killed? She vaguely wondered how Morning Song was getting along with the baby, but her fear for Isaac's safety wouldn't allow her to leave the little knot of ladies clustered together in a camaraderie of fearful waiting.

Emmie started to her feet at the sound of a shout outside. She threw her cloak around herself and rushed to the door, followed by the rest of the ladies. She ran toward the gate as doors opened and wagons creaked inside. Dead bodies were heaped on the wagons, but she couldn't look at them. Isaac couldn't be in that number. She searched the mounted men for a glimpse of Isaac's dear face. She exhaled when she saw Rand, Jacob, and Isaac clustered near the last wagon.

Emmie waited with the other ladies near the flagpole, and Captain Ten Eyck stopped just a few feet away from them where Colonel Carrington stood.

His salute was a short, tired wave. "Sir, I'm sorry to report that Fetterman's entire command has been massacred. I brought in all I could, about forty-nine, but there are still more to be claimed."

Frances gasped and started to slide to the ground in a near faint as the ladies overheard Captain Ten Eyck's words. Emmie caught her by the elbow, and she rallied before bursting into tears.

"I knew it," she sobbed. "I just knew he was dead."

Mrs. Carrington put her arms

around Frances. "You're coming home with me, dear." She led her away.

Sarah tugged Emmie's arm. "Let's go home."

Emmie saw the dark circles under Sarah's eyes. Her pallor was so pronounced she looked as though she might pass out at any moment. "You're going right home to bed." She took Sarah's arm and steadied her against the wind as they made their way toward their home.

The fire was out when they finally pushed the door shut against the wind. Emmie hurried to start one while Sarah poked the fire in the kitchen stove to life.

"I'm going to put on some water for tea," Sarah said. "I can't go to bed until Rand gets home. I couldn't rest anyway until I know what happened."

Joel came in moments later, his young face sober. He silently heaped wood in the fireplace for Emmie, then sat on the floor with his knees drawn up to his chin. The news had squelched even his high spirits.

By the time the men arrived, warm currents from the fire heated the room, and the aroma of steeping tea filled the kitchen. Emmie cut some thick slabs of bread and spread butter and jam on them. She was suddenly ravenous and knew the men would be too. Morning Song was still at Jacob's. The weather was much too cold to have the baby out, but she wished for Morning Song's calming presence. Did she know what had happened? And was she even safe? The anger against the Sioux would be ready to boil over with this news.

The door opened and Rand and Isaac dashed in before slamming it against the howling wind. Sarah uttered a little cry and flew into Rand's arms. Emmie was right behind her as she ran to Isaac. She buried her face in the rough wool of his coat and burst into tears.

He put his lips against her hair and patted her on the back. "We're okay."

Emmie pulled away and looked up at him. "I'm sorry." What was she thinking of? She had no right to be in Isaac's arms.

Isaac held on a moment, then let her go. "It's not over yet. I still intend to talk to Jacob."

Emmie nodded. "Want some tea and bread?"

"I thought you'd never ask," Isaac said. "I could eat the whole loaf. I'm famished."

"Me too." Rand walked toward the kitchen with his arm around his wife.

"Where's Jacob?" Sarah asked. "I thought he would come to see that Emmie was all right. After all, he says he wants to marry her."

"He wanted to see about Gabrielle," Rand said.

Emmie glanced at Isaac. He had come to find her as soon as he could, but Jacob hadn't. This was just a taste of what it would be like to be married to a man who didn't love her. Not that she wanted Jacob to love her. She couldn't imagine dealing with that problem too.

Sarah sniffed. "Is he coming over later?"

"No," Rand said. "He said he'd see us in the morning. We're all beat."

Sarah's fierce look softened. "Tell us about it."

They spent the next hour exclaiming over the harrowing adventure as Rand and Isaac related the day's events.

"I wish you would have asked Wolverine about White Dove," Sarah said. "I would love to see her again."

"And what about Red Hawk?" Joel put in eagerly. "Did you see him?"

Rand shook his head. "I didn't see Red Hawk and it would have done no good to ask about White Dove. Even if she were close, you couldn't see her, sweetheart. It's too dangerous to set foot outside the fort. You know that. You haven't been outside the gate since we got here."

"I still wish you'd asked. I'd like to know she's all right."

Rand grinned. "Well, if we ever get in that situation, I'll be sure to say that my wife has insisted on knowing where his woman is. He'll be very impressed."

Sarah chuckled, then stood. "I'm going to bed. I'll fall asleep right here in this chair if I don't go now." She put her hand on her brother's shoulder. "You'd better get to bed too, Joel." He didn't complain but went off to his cot in the parlor.

Rand yawned. "Me too. See you all tomorrow." He stood and followed his wife into the bedroom and shut the door.

"I should be going too," Isaac said. "It's been a long day."

Emmie stood and followed him to the door.

"Try not to worry." He bent and kissed her on the forehead. "Things will be all right. I'm going to build us a home. I promise."

118

Emmie shut the door behind him. She just didn't see any way out.

Six

The next morning Emmie hurried across the parade ground toward the Carrington residence. It was hard to keep her balance in the driving wind. Already four inches of snow had fallen, and if she didn't check on Frances soon, she might not be able to get through the drifts.

A pall of dread and foreboding hung over the little fort. She saw sober faces everywhere she looked. The biggest danger, Rand had said, was that the Sioux would attack the fort itself. Only the Indians' fear of the big howitzers kept them at bay. If they did attack, all would be lost because the soldiers were outnumbered and low on ammunition.

Frances was huddled in a quilt on the sofa by the fire when Mrs. Carrington ushered Emmie into the parlor. Frances was pale, but she seemed composed with a strange peace.

"I somehow knew it would come to this," she told Emmie. "George seemed determined to force a fight with the Indians. He idolized Fetterman, but I knew his rashness would come to a bad end. George just wouldn't see it."

Someone knocked at the door

again, and Sample, the Carrington's orderly, led in a bearded man in his thirties. He was dressed in civilian clothes and had a wolf robe over his shoulder. He took off his hat and stood, turning it in his hands in front of Frances.

"Miz Grummond. My name is John Phillips. I been a miner and a scout, but I ain't never seen such a bad thing. You been through enough. I'm goin' to Laramie for help for your sake if it costs me my life." He pulled the robe from his shoulder and laid it across Frances's lap. "Here is my wolf robe. I want you to have it to remember me by if I don't make it back."

Frances was nearly speechless, but then she thanked him with tears in her eyes as she stroked the robe.

"Are you going alone?" Emmie asked him.

He shook his head. "Lieutenant Liddle has asked to go too. We're setting out at different times, though. If one of us don't make it, maybe the other one will get through."

Isaac was going out through a blinding blizzard surrounded by hostile Indians? Why didn't he tell her that last night?

Emmie fought to maintain her composure. "I must go."

Everyone was assembled in the parlor when she arrived at the Campbell house. Jacob glanced at her when she came in, then quickly looked away. Isaac, his face set in a stubborn mask, stood stiffly with his back against the fireplace mantel. Sarah looked as though she had been crying.

"So it's true!" Emmie burst out. "You're going to Fort Laramie."

"Someone has to go," Isaac said. "We can't just send Phillips and hope he makes it. Too much is at stake. We have to have reinforcements and ammo. If the Sioux attack, we'll lose the fort itself and everyone in it."

"He's right," Rand said. "Wolverine said the Sioux are planning to attack soon. We can't afford to wait and just hope headquarters will send the reinforcements Colonel Carrington has been requesting for months now."

Emmie's eyes burned, but she refused to make it harder on Isaac by crying. "But why does it have to be you?"

"Why not me? I don't have a wife and children here like some of the other men. And I know this terrain. I have to try." A bugle sounded at the other end of the fort. "That's assembly. We have to go."

The men all put on their coats and filed out the door. Emmie wanted to run and fling her arms around Isaac one last time, but how could she with Jacob there? What if she never saw Isaac again? She struggled against the tears as the door shut against the howling wind. She whispered a prayer for Isaac's safety as she watched his retreating back through the window.

The blizzard had intensified as Isaac, followed by Rand and Jacob, fought the wind all the way across the parade ground. John Phillips had already gone ahead to summon relief from Fort Laramie, and Isaac wanted to get on his way. He was about to mount up when Jacob approached him with a determined look on his face.

"I need to speak with you before you go."

Isaac turned and faced his friend. He had tried to hate him for what Jacob was doing to him and Emmie, but he couldn't. All Isaac could feel was compassion and pity.

"I know I've been acting like a fool," Jacob said. "My brother has been none too gentle about pointing it out to me. I want you to know before you go that I'm releasing Emmie from her promise — if you make it back." He grinned and thrust out his hand. "That's good incentive for you to fight to get through."

Isaac let out the breath he had been holding. "Thank you." He took Jake's hand and pumped it.

A shadow darkened Jake's face. "Amelia would be ashamed of me. I've struggled with this thing every night. God wouldn't let me sleep or eat. He just kept telling me like he told Job, 'Where were you when I laid the foundations of the earth?'

I don't understand why he would take the one person who gave my life meaning without even letting me say good-bye." Tears glistened in his eyes and he swallowed hard.

"What will you do with Gabrielle? She still needs a mother." Isaac hesitated, then plunged ahead. "We would be willing to raise her."

"No, but thanks. I'm going to marry Morning Song."

Isaac's eyes widened. "Have you asked her?"

"Not yet, but she loves Gabrielle." Jacob wore a sad smile. "And her John needs a father." He clapped Isaac on the back. "I don't want to say anything until you get back. If you don't make it, Emmie's baby will need a father and I will honor my promise to Amelia." He said this last with a defiant determination.

"Agreed. I would want her taken care of." Isaac gripped Jacob's hand again. "Whatever happens, will you promise me you will try to learn to love your new wife? Amelia wouldn't want you to marry just for convenience. She intended for you to be happy."

Jacob was silent a moment, then returned the pressure of Isaac's fingers. "I don't see how I can ever love anyone but Amelia, but I will try."

"That's all I ask." The two men looked at one another a moment. "Take care, Jacob."

Jacob nodded. "I'll be careful.

And Godspeed, my friend."

With a last handshake, Isaac swung up onto Buck and urged him toward the gate. He heard a cry behind him and turned to see Emmie running across the parade ground toward him with her navy cloak flying behind her in the wind. He dismounted and caught her in his arms.

"Be safe." She cupped his cheeks in her gloved hands and reached up to kiss him.

The touch of her lips on his and the sweet scent of her breath on his face warmed him clear through. He kissed her for a long moment, then pulled away to stare into her face. "It's going to be all right, Emmie. Jacob has released you. I have every reason to get through and bring relief to the fort. Don't give up on me, no matter what."

Tears sparkled in her violet-blue eyes. "I won't. I'll be waiting for you."

A soldier opened the gate and saluted as Isaac slipped outside into the blinding snow. He had thought long and hard about what would be the best way to accomplish his mission. He decided to avoid obvious trails and travel by night as much as possible. That would help keep him warm during the frigid nights, and he could avoid confrontation with the Indians. He had left by a back gate and counted on the Sioux being occupied with celebrating their victory. The detail of men riding out to retrieve the dead would divert the Indians also.

The blizzard intensified out on the plain with no fort walls to block the wind. Isaac's mustache was soon coated with snow and ice, and he wished he had a full beard like many of the men wore. He had to stop often and walk his horse through the snowdrifts. It had to be at least twenty or thirty below zero even without the wind.

He found it hard to stay awake as he clung to the pommel. The wind cut through even his buffalo robe, and he swayed in the saddle. He had to hang on and get help for Emmie and his friends. Clutching the pommel with both hands, he fought to stay mounted.

As his horse rounded a grove of trees, he lost his tenuous grip and pitched sideways from the saddle into a drift. He felt nice and warm away from the wind. He'd just lay here and get warm for a few minutes. He closed his eyes and slid into unconsciousness.

SEVEN

Emmie awoke near dawn on Christmas Eve to a cold room with the fire out. Isaac had been gone three days. He hadn't had a fire or shelter in all that time.

The sentry's cry came. "Five o'clock and all's well."

All's well. No one really believed that. The mood at the fort had been a peculiar one the last few days. Everyone seemed on edge as though they were listening for some sound beyond the log walls of the stockade. Rand and Jacob along with their detachment had come back two days ago with the rest of the bodies of the slain soldiers. The Sioux hadn't bothered them at all. Rand said he wasn't sure if they were holed up in camp because of the blizzard or simply too busy celebrating their victory.

Jacob told them that before they left to recover the bodies, Colonel Carrington had opened the magazine and cut the Bormann fuses of round case shot. He opened the boxes of ammunition and adjusted them so that by lighting a single match, the whole lot would go up. His instructions were that if the Indians attacked in overwhelming numbers, the women and children were to be put in the magazine and blown up rather than have any captured alive. Thankfully, that had not happened, but Emmie couldn't forget that the magazine was still readied for such an eventuality.

It had taken several days to dig the grave site in the frozen ground for the slain men. It was so cold the men could only work in fifteen-minute shifts.

Joel voiced all their fears when he innocently remarked, "How come they can only work for fifteen minutes when Isaac and John are out in the wind all the time?"

Emmie wondered the same thing. The snowstorm would subside for a few hours, and then the snow would swirl down again in a blinding curtain. The soldiers had done all they could to keep a ten-foot trench dug around the stockade. If they had allowed the drifts to pile up, the Indians could have walked right over the tops of the logs in the stockade.

Normally today they would be wrapping presents and preparing food for a feast on Christmas day. She sighed and slipped out of bed to get the fire going, then pulled on her warmest dress, the worn blue wool one, and quickly combed her hair and washed her face in the cracked bowl on the stand by her bed.

She could try to make Christmas a little festive for Joel and Sarah. She would go to Jacob's and check on Gabrielle, then see about what she could use for a tree. There were none on the fort grounds, but maybe Joel could find her a branch or something. Joel had been staying at Jacob's for appearance's sake, so Morning Song could take care of the baby. The added benefit of her staying at Jacob's was her safety. There had been a few pointed remarks flung her way by some of the survivors of the massacre.

Emmie had caught Morning Song staring at Jacob with a longing expression a few times and hoped the young woman wasn't headed for heartbreak. Jacob was still too buttoned up by grief to notice another woman.

By the time Sarah and Rand came into the kitchen, the room had lost its chill. Emmie looked up as Sarah sat next to her and pulled the teapot over to pour a cup of tea. Rand sat next to Sarah to pull on his boots.

Emmie studied Sarah's drawn face. "You look as though you haven't slept all night."

Sarah sighed. "I'm feeling a bit poorly. My back hurts strangely. The pain seems to come and go."

Emmie narrowed her eyes and looked Sarah over. "I think perhaps Dr. Horton ought to take a look at you. It could be the baby."

Rand reared his head abruptly. "The baby? It isn't time yet."

"Not quite," Emmie said. "But

it's not unusual for one to make his appearance a few weeks early."

"I'll get the doc." Rand grabbed his greatcoat and hurried out the door.

Sarah put her hand to her back. "I did wonder. But I didn't want it to be the baby yet. I'm afraid, Emmie." Tears pooled in her eyes as she looked up. "I don't want to leave Rand and my baby. What if something goes wrong?"

Emmie's chest felt heavy, and she shook her head. "Don't talk like that. Nothing is going to go wrong. Now you go get undressed and climb into bed so the doctor can check you."

Sarah nodded and went to the bedroom. A few minutes later Rand

and Dr. Horton opened the door and hurried inside. Both were red faced from the biting wind. Rand's brown mustache and the doctor's beard were coated with snow. Dr. Horton tapped on the bedroom door and went right in.

Rand stared blankly at the shut door, then sank onto a chair. "I'm so afraid, Emmie. What if — ?" He broke off his words in midsentence.

"Sarah is strong. She'll be fine." Emmie had to cling to that belief.

They sat in silence until the doctor opened the door and came back into the kitchen. "The baby's coming. Unfortunately Sarah is having back labor, so she'll be uncomfortable. It may help to rub her back, or she may not want you to touch her. It varies from woman to woman. I'll check back in a couple of hours. If the situation changes, send for me."

He left a small bottle of laudanum with them in case the pain got worse. When the door closed behind him, Emmie and Rand went to the bedroom.

Sarah bore a wan smile and held out her hand for Emmie. "You were right."

Emmie squeezed her hand. "The doctor says it will be a while yet, so try to rest while you can. We all may have a wonderful Christmas present after all."

"Oh, I hope it doesn't take that long." Sarah moaned as she burrowed deeper under the covers.

Rand and Emmie tiptoed out of the room and shut the door behind them. "I'll run over and tell Jacob and Joel," Rand said. "Morning Song will want to be here too. And we may need her."

Emmie nodded. "It wouldn't hurt for Jacob to keep you company."

Rand grimaced. "He may not be able to stand it after losing Amelia." He went toward the door. "If Sarah wakes up and asks for me, tell her I'll be right back."

She sighed and sat at the table. A thousand "what ifs" rang in her head. What if she lost both Isaac and Sarah? She shuddered at the thought. Even losing one would devastate her. She just couldn't think about it. She stood. She would keep busy and the day would soon be over. The baby would be here and soon there would be news of Isaac.

By the time she had cleaned the kitchen, Rand was back. Jacob, Morning Song, and Joel were with him. Jacob had baby Gabrielle wrapped up in a buffalo robe, and her blue eyes peered up at her surroundings as soon as her father unwrapped her. Joel carried John over and set him down to play by a bucket of toys on the rug near the fire.

Morning Song took off her cloak and hurried to the bedroom to check on Sarah. "She is still sleeping," she announced when she came back out. "That is good. She will need strength."

Emmie walked over to Jacob and held out her arms for the baby. Jacob kissed his daughter's fuzzy head, then handed her to Emmie and went to sit beside his brother. Everyone seemed quiet and subdued, and Amelia's spirit seemed to hover very near. Emmie knew no one could forget the terrible outcome of Gabrielle's birth. As she cuddled the baby, her own baby moved for the first time in her womb. She gulped and pressed a hand to her stomach.

Tears pricked her eyes as she thought about what the future held for her and her baby. Everything was such a mess.

Through the long day Sarah's

pains gradually intensified. Joel kept little John occupied while Morning Song and Emmie took turns caring for Gabrielle and tending to Sarah.

Dr. Horton popped in several times to check on Sarah's progress. "It will be a while," he kept saying.

Rand and Jacob grew quieter and more strained as the day wore on. Several times when Emmie came out of the bedroom, she saw them with their heads bent in prayer. The wind, howling around the corners of the house and whistling through the cracks around the doors and windows, put everyone on edge.

After supper Sarah's labor began in earnest. With Rand on one side and Emmie hovering behind him,

Dr. Horton tried to give her a small dose of laudanum.

She shook her head. "I don't want to risk any harm to the baby."

He snorted, but he put his bottle away without protest.

Sarah did not let out one cry when the pains came but only gripped Emmie's hand tighter. An occasional soft groan passed her lips. By ten o'clock the doctor had settled in with them for the night.

"It could be any time," he said finally.

Morning Song fed Gabrielle one last time and put her down for the night, then pulled up a chair beside her friend's bed. "Baby will come soon now." She and Emmie took turns bathing Sarah's face with a wet cloth and rubbing her back during the contractions.

Just after midnight on Christmas day, Sarah gave one last mighty push, and a tiny baby boy slid into the world. He squalled in protest when Dr. Horton wiped the mucus away from his nose and mouth. Emmie grinned at the strong, lusty protest. She wrapped him in a bit of flannel and laid him in Sarah's arms.

Sarah stroked a finger down his cheek. "Isn't he beautiful? He looks just like his daddy."

"I'll get Rand now." Emmie closed the door behind her and found Rand just outside the door. Joel and John were asleep on a rug by the fire. Jacob sat at the table with his head in his hands. He and Rand looked pale and haggard.

"You have a beautiful son," Emmie said with a smile. "Do you want to see him?"

"How's Sarah?" Rand asked urgently.

"Tired, but just as beautiful as ever."

"Thank God," Jacob murmured.

Rand shot through the door, and Sarah cried out and held out her arms to him. He went down on his knees by the bed and buried his face in her hair. She patted him and winked at Emmie, who closed the door behind Morning Song and the doctor.

Jacob's knuckles were white as he gripped the table. "I have to go now." He grabbed his greatcoat and ran out into the howling wind.

"Wait, Jacob," Emmie called, but he just kept on going. She blinked back tears — there was such pain and grief in his eyes.

Morning Song looked at the door for a moment, then bundled the baby up. "I go home with the baby." She wrapped her cloak around her. "Send John home with Joel in morning."

Emmie was too tired to protest at the way it would look if Morning Song spent the night at Jacob's alone with him. He probably wouldn't be there anyway but would likely be at Amelia's grave site.

Rand opened the door and

stepped into the kitchen with his small son in his arms. "He seems big and healthy in spite of coming early." He glanced around. "Where's Jacob?"

"He had to leave. I think it was too much for him." Emmie hurried to him and held out her arms for the tiny scrapper. "I think he needs to be cleaned up a bit."

She had readied some warm water and strips of soft flannel. She had Rand pull the kitchen table close to the stove to keep the baby warm, and she quickly cleaned the little one and popped him into a gown. He was awake but made no protest at her ministrations. She wrapped him in a flannel blanket and handed him back to his father, who took him eagerly.

Rand gazed down into the face of his son with a look of awe and pride. "Sarah says he looks like me. But I don't see it."

Emmie laughed. "Then you must be blind. Look at that nose. And he has your dimples."

Just then the baby yawned and moved his mouth in such a way that Rand saw his dimples for the first time. "Ma will be so excited to hear about him."

"Maybe your family can come for a visit soon. This may be all it takes to heal the breach with your father."

A shadow darkened Rand's brow. "I wouldn't hold my breath. Pa is determined that I give up what he calls my foolishness and come back to the farm. Ma says he doesn't mention my name."

"A grandchild can change everything."

"Maybe." Rand shrugged.

There was a sound from the parlor, and Joel came flying into the kitchen. His reddish-gold hair stood on end as he slid to a stop in front of Rand and the baby. "Let me see."

Rand grinned and pulled back the blanket to reveal the baby. "Meet your new nephew."

Joel gave a sigh of awe. "Can I hold him?"

Rand passed him over to the young boy. "He's going to be pestering you unmercifully before you know it."

"I'm going to be the best uncle there ever was," Joel promised in a hushed tone. "I'm going to teach him all kinds of things, like where the best fishing spot is and how to play baseball." He looked up from his perusal of his nephew with a sudden look of alarm. "How's Sarah? She's all right, isn't she?"

Rand nodded toward the bedroom door. "See for yourself."

Joel carried the baby to the bedroom as Emmie opened the door for him. Sarah looked asleep, but she opened her eyes as soon as Joel stepped into the room. She smiled when she saw her brother with her baby. "Did Rand tell you what we named him?"

Joel shook his head. "I forgot to ask," he said with a sheepish look.

Sarah laughed. "His name is Joshua Joel Campbell."

Joel gaped, and his chest swelled. "Man alive. If that don't beat the dutch."

Rand clapped a hand on his shoulder. "If he turns out as good a boy as his namesake, we'll be very pleased."

Tears welled up in Joel's eyes at such praise from the man he adored. "I'll try to be a good example."

Sarah yawned, and Emmie saw her weariness. "It's time for the new mama to get some rest." She shooed everyone out of the bedroom and put little Joshua in his cradle.

Sarah smiled sleepily at her as Emmie plumped the pillows and straightened the covers. "I did well, didn't I?"

"You did very well." Emmie kissed her forehead. "We're all very proud of you."

Sarah smiled again and was asleep before Emmie could leave the room.

EIGHT

Two days into the new year, Emmie sat at the kitchen table up to her elbows in flour as she kneaded bread while Sarah nursed the baby. Emmie froze as the bugle sounded the long roll that meant troops had been spotted. Her hand to her breast, she held her breath as she rose and listened more closely. The bugle sounded again and she bolted toward the door.

"Stay there," she told Sarah as she threw her cloak around her and ran out the door. From every home, people poured out the doors with looks of dawning hope. Jacob ran past her and she grabbed at his arm.

"Fresh troops are almost here," he told her. "Phillips or Isaac made it through!"

Tears of relief flooded her eyes as she ran to stand beside Frances. Even Jessica and her mother were out. Jessica saw her stare and turned away. The troops flooded through the gates. They all looked nearly frozen. Most had frostbite patches of white on their cheeks, their mustaches and beards were thickly caked with snow and ice, and they all wore a look of intense suffering. Desperate to find Isaac, she looked frantically through the milling men and horses, but there was no familiar grin or shock of auburn hair.

Colonel Carrington stood off to one side, talking to the major who had led the men. After several minutes, he came to where the women were. "Phillips made it through on Christmas day. It has taken this long for them to get through the blizzard."

Emmie caught at his arm. "What about Isaac?"

Colonel Carrington shook his head. "I'm sorry, my dear. He never showed up at the fort."

Emmie caught her breath. She clenched her hands beneath the folds of her cloak. He must be mistaken. Of course Isaac made it through. He was wrong. She searched the colonel's face, but she saw only compassion and understanding.

She took a step back. "No, you're wrong." She turned and ran across the parade ground. She'd find Rand. He'd know the truth. She found him giving directions to the men assigned to unpack the stores of supplies the troops had brought.

"Rand, I can't find any news of Isaac."

He put an arm around her and drew her off to one side. She looked up into his brown eyes and saw grief.

She put her hands on his chest and pushed. "He's not dead. I'd know if he were dead. He promised he'd come back. We're going to build a life together. Our own home . . ."

Rand pulled her to him and held her. "You're strong now, Emmie, and you've got to face the facts. He didn't make it. He was a brave soldier, and he'd want you to be brave now too."

She wept against the rough wool of his jacket, but everything felt unreal. Isaac couldn't be dead. She couldn't accept that. "I promised I'd wait, and I will. He'll come back. You'll see."

"Let me take you home." Rand led her across the parade ground as she walked woodenly back to their quarters. Sarah glanced up as she came in and stood with a cry. She held out her arms and Emmie flew into them.

His face grim, Jacob stepped out from behind Rand. "Our marriage can go forward, Emmie. I'll make sure you and your baby are all right like I promised Amelia."

She shook her head. "No, Jacob. You released me. I'm going to wait for Isaac to return." She ignored the pity in his eyes as he turned away.

Isaac stirred and licked his lips. He was so thirsty. He sat up and stared at the fireplace across the room. Where was he? The last thing he clearly remembered was pitching into a snowbank. He had vague impressions of the dark face of an old man that swam in and out of sight and dim memories of tossing and crying out feverishly.

A door opened and the man in Isaac's dreams came through it. He was short and husky with a beard clear to his chest and black matted hair. He wore a faded red flannel shirt, stained and patched in numerous places, and trousers so dirty it was hard to tell what their original color had been. He squinted at Isaac, then spat a stream of tobacco juice on the floor.

"Awake, are you?" He scowled. "What in tarnation were you doing wandering around in a blizzard?"

Isaac struggled to swing his feet

over the edge of the cot. "What day is it?"

"Don't believe in answering questions? That ain't polite."

"I've got to get to Fort Laramie. It's a matter of life and death." Isaac stood and swayed weakly. He leaned against the wall until his head stopped spinning.

"It was pert' near your death. You was as close to freezing to death as I'd ever seen. And the fever that followed about finished the job. It's a ways to Laramie. What's so all fired important? I can see you're a soldier."

Isaac nodded. "There's been a bloody massacre at Fort Phil Kearny. We need ammo and men, or we'll lose the fort itself and every man, woman, and child in it." He sat back down on the edge of the cot. "Where's my horse?"

"Not so fast. You can't light out again without some vittles. All you've eaten is a little broth I was able to get down you. You'd never make it past the corral." He pointed to the table. "Sit down and fill your belly. The wind is still screaming like a banshee. The soup will warm you."

Isaac eyed the steaming bowl. He was ravenous. He started toward the table and staggered. What was wrong with him? He sank into the chair.

The man cackled and pushed the bowl of stew toward Isaac. "My name's Pete Sweeney but folks call me Hardtack. I reckon 'cause they think I'm as tough as old shoe leather."

Isaac picked up a bent and tarnished spoon and dug into the stew. The smell made his mouth water. "Lieutenant Liddle," he mumbled between bites. "How far are we from Fort Laramie?"

" 'Bout a day's ride on a fresh horse. Which your horse ain't. He was as near dead as you. Just now startin' to perk up some."

"You got a fresh horse?" Isaac wiped up the last of the stew with a crust of bread and stood.

"Naw. I got an old mule named Bertha, and she ain't good for much but carrying a light load downhill. She'd never make it to

Laramie."

"What day is it?" Isaac asked again.

Hardtack scratched his grizzled head. "I don't rightly know. The days all run together out here." He stood and walked to a faded, dirty calendar nailed to the wall by the door. "Let's see, this is the day I went for supplies, and it took me seven days coming back. I found you here and that were six days ago."

"Six days! I've been here six days?"

The old man continued as though Isaac had not interrupted. "January second. Near as I can figure."

"I've got to get to Laramie." Isaac jumped to his feet and looked around. "Where're my boots?"

Hardtack pointed a gnarled finger. "Under the bed."

Isaac grabbed his boots and feverishly began to pull them on. "I even missed Christmas." He'd had such special plans for Emmie. His mother's engagement ring was hidden back in his room, waiting for the right moment to give it to her. "I have to get reinforcements." He began to search for his greatcoat and buffalo robe.

Hardtack sighed and pointed to the other side of the bed. "If you're bent on killing yourself and your horse, I reckon I can't stop you."

Isaac thanked the old man again, then hurried outside. He staggered weakly through the drifts of snow to the shed surrounded by a rickety corral. He found Buck bedded down in a heap of straw with an old blanket thrown over him.

"Sorry, boy. We've got to get on the road again."

He slipped the bit into Buck's mouth and hurriedly saddled him. He led him out the door into the wind-driven snow. After swinging up into the saddle, he tucked his buffalo robe securely around him, checked his compass, and dug his heels into Buck's flank.

He was close enough to Fort Laramie to travel in the daylight. This close to the fort most of the Indians were friendly Brulé Sioux. It was still slow going in the drifting snow, but Isaac felt a new strength coursing through him, a new optimism. He was going to make it.

After riding nearly three hours, he began to recognize the terrain. He was almost to Fort Laramie. Maybe they would have news of Fort Phil Kearny. A sentry stopped him as he rode up, then opened the gate. Isaac made his way to the commanding officer's headquarters and knocked on the door.

"Enter," the commander called.

He stepped inside and saluted the major seated behind a scarred makeshift desk. "Sir, I come with a dispatch from Colonel Carrington at Fort Phil Kearny. There's been a terrible battle and we desperately need reinforcements and ammunition."

The major waved his hand. "Where have you been, Lieutenant? We got word of the massacre days ago. Troops should just about be there by now."

Isaac sagged in relief. The fort was saved. "I had some bad luck, Major. I'm just thankful Phillips made it through."

The major nodded. "You don't look well, Lieutenant. You'd better head to mess and get some chow."

Isaac opened his mouth to object and say he was going back to Fort Phil Kearny, when the major interrupted him.

"That's an order, Lieutenant."

Isaac sighed. It seemed he didn't have a choice. He saluted, then left headquarters and made his way across the tiny parade ground to the mess hall. After a bowl of stew and a stringy piece of meat, he mounted up and pointed Buck's head back to Fort Phil Kearny.

Reveille sounded outside in the parade ground. Two weeks. Emmie put water on to boil for soup and tried to hold on to hope that Isaac had survived the trip, but he'd never made it back to the fort.

He can't be dead. I won't believe it.

Sunshine blazed through the windows and shone on the wooden table as she opened some canned vegetables for the soup. She pulled out a chair and sat down with her back to the door. She could hear

Sarah singing to Amelia's baby in the bedroom.

The door creaked behind her, and a cold wind rushed in. "Emmie."

She froze, almost afraid to turn at the deep timbres of Isaac's voice. Maybe she was dreaming. She turned at his touch and looked up into his dear face. His mustache had grown into a beard during the time he'd been gone, and he looked gaunt. But his blue eyes sparkled with joy, and his lips turned up in a tender smile.

"I-Isaac?" She reached up to touch his face, and the rough scratch of his beard assured her that she was awake. "They said you'd died in the blizzard."

"I'm too tough even for a blizzard. If you're marrying anyone, it had better be me."

She finally looked over his shoulder and saw Rand and Jacob standing in the doorway. Both were grinning. She clutched his hand and stared into his face. "Isaac?" Blinking, she let her gaze travel over the planes and contours of his face, rough and reddened by exposure. She rose from the table and threw herself into his arms. "Isaac!"

The feel of his arms around her and the sensation of the coarse wool under her cheek grounded her in the moment. He was really here.

"What's going on?" Sarah stood in the doorway with the baby in her arms. Her eyes widened when she saw Isaac. "Oh, Isaac, you're alive!"

Rand stepped past him and Jacob shut the back door.

Emmie pulled her face out of Isaac's wool coat. "Are you all right?"

"I am now." His voice was husky as he hugged her. "Sorry I didn't make it back sooner. I know you were worried."

She glanced at Jacob to see how he was taking the upheaval of his plans, but he was staring at Morning Song who looked back at him with her heart in her eyes. Emmie blinked and realized that Morning Song cared about Jacob. No one could ever replace Amelia, but maybe Jacob could heal in time.

Emmie looked back at Isaac and laid her head against his chest again. His pulse thumped strongly under her ear, and she wound her arms around his waist. "Are you all right, truly?"

He rested his head atop her head. "Not even any frostbite."

"Where have you been all this time? How did you survive the blizzard on your own?"

"I wasn't alone. God was with me even in the storm. This old geezer stumbled across me when I couldn't go any farther, but we both know who directed his steps." He pulled away a moment and cupped her face in his cold hands. "I couldn't wait to get home to you."

She closed her eyes as his lips came down on hers. The cold encasing her heart melted into warmth that spread through her midsection. Isaac's love had made her whole. Their future together stretched in front of them as brightly as the sun sparkling on the snow.

EPILOGUE

Emmie looked around the nearly bare rooms where she'd spent the last two years. Was she leaving anything behind? This would be the last time she would ever see these rooms again. Sap no longer oozed from the rough logs, and the tiny rooms looked barren without their gay calico curtains and tablecloths. Dust motes danced in the hot summer sunshine that filled the parlor.

The treaty of 1868 had agreed to abandon Forts Reno, C.F. Smith, and Phil Kearny to the Indians. No one would ever inhabit these walls again. Isaac said the Indians would burn the fort as soon as the soldiers were out of sight. Jessica had already left to go to Fort Laramie with her mother, and the rest of them would leave for various locations too.

She looked down at a tug on her skirt. Tiny Amelia, just over two, lifted her arms up to be held. Smiling, Emmie knelt and took the child in her arms. She buried her face in her daughter's sweet-smelling hair. God had blessed her so much. Amelia's birth had been easy, and the joy the little girl brought to both Isaac and her was simply amazing. Who would have thought Emmie would have so much just three years after she had heard the shriek of the overturning carriage that day in Wabash?

Life was good. Even Jake seemed to have finally put the past behind him. He looked at Morning Song with love in his eyes now. They were expecting an addition to their little family in October. Sarah had given Rand another son last year and was also expecting a new baby around Christmas. She and Rand had said they wanted a large family, and they were well on their way to having their dreams fulfilled. Emmie had even had an opportunity to tell her brother, Labe, about how God had changed her life when he'd stopped by three months ago on his way back to the gold fields of Bozeman.

He had brought news about Ben's death in a shooting during a poker game with other miners. Emmie had been sad but not surprised. Ben had too much pride to ever bend his knee to God.

Emmie whirled now as the front door banged shut and her husband strode in. Isaac smiled as he caught sight of her with Amelia in her arms.

"It won't be long before you won't be able to pick her up." He glanced at the gentle bulge where their new baby grew. Amelia held out her arms to him, and he took her and tossed her into the air.

She giggled. "Again, Daddy!"

Emmie watched as Isaac played with Amelia. He was never too busy to take a moment to bring a smile to the little girl's face. He had certainly kept his promise to be a good father. And husband. She loved him with a fierce, almost painful love.

His deep voice interrupted her introspection. "Are you ready to leave?"

Emmie linked her arm through his and gazed up into his blue eyes. "I'm ready." He opened the door and they walked across the parade ground for the last time.

"Bye, bye, house." Little Amelia waved her chubby hands.

Emmie echoed the sentiment in her heart as Isaac helped her up into their wagon and then handed Amelia to her. A new home awaited them near Sheridan . . . Home. Isaac was everything the word meant to her. And no matter where they were, as long as he was with her, she was home.

ABOUT THE AUTHOR

RITA finalist **Colleen Coble** is the author of several bestselling romantic suspense novels, including *Tidewater Inn,* and the Mercy Falls, Lonestar, and Rock Harbor series.